Cinderella's Dream Wedding

By Susan Amerikaner

Illustrated by Gabriella Matta, Mario Cortes, and Studio IBOIX

Random House New York

Copyright © 2012 Disney Enterprises, Inc. All rights reserved. Published in the United States by Random House Children's Books, a division of Random House, Inc., 1745 Broadway, New York, NY 10019, and in Canada by Random House of Canada Limited, Toronto, in conjunction with Disney Enterprises, Inc. Random House and the colophon are registered trademarks of Random House, Inc.

ISBN: 978-0-7364-2910-8

randomhouse.com/kids

MANUFACTURED IN CHINA

10 9 8 7 6 5 4 3 2 1

Prince Charming had found the woman of his dreams. He couldn't wait to make Cinderella his wife.

The Prince bent down on one knee and held out a diamond ring. "Will you marry me?" he asked Cinderella.

"Yes!" cried Cinderella as she jumped into the Prince's arms.

The first person to hear the good news was the King. He showed the happy couple a painting of his wife on their wedding day. "Cinderella shall wear the same outfit," the King explained. "It is a royal family tradition."

Cinderella did not want to disappoint the King, but there were problems with the Queen's wedding dress. It did not fit well. And the pearl necklace the Queen had worn was so big and heavy, it pulled poor Cinderella down to the ground!

Cinderella had an idea. She showed a portrait of her mother on her wedding day to the royal dressmaker. "The Fairy Godmother is making me a dress just like this. Could you add special stitching to the hem in the Queen's favorite color?" she asked.

"It would be an honor," replied the dressmaker.

Soon after, Cinderella visited the royal jeweler. She handed him the pearl necklace and a choker with a heart-shaped jewel her mother had given her many years ago. "Do you think you can combine these into one necklace?" asked Cinderella.

The jeweler promised to do his finest work.

The royal wedding day arrived. Cinderella's gown and necklace looked beautiful. And she had sewn the extra pearls onto her veil!

"I'm wearing a copy of my mother's dress to honor my family," she explained to the King. "And with my newly designed necklace and veil, I also honor your family's tradition."

The King smiled. "How wonderful!" he exclaimed. "You have blended the treasures of two families— and created a new tradition."

The King proudly offered Cinderella his arm and led her down the aisle. "Let's not keep the Prince waiting."

The wedding ceremony was magical! Cinderella and the Prince were thrilled to have all their friends and family in attendance as they became husband and wife.

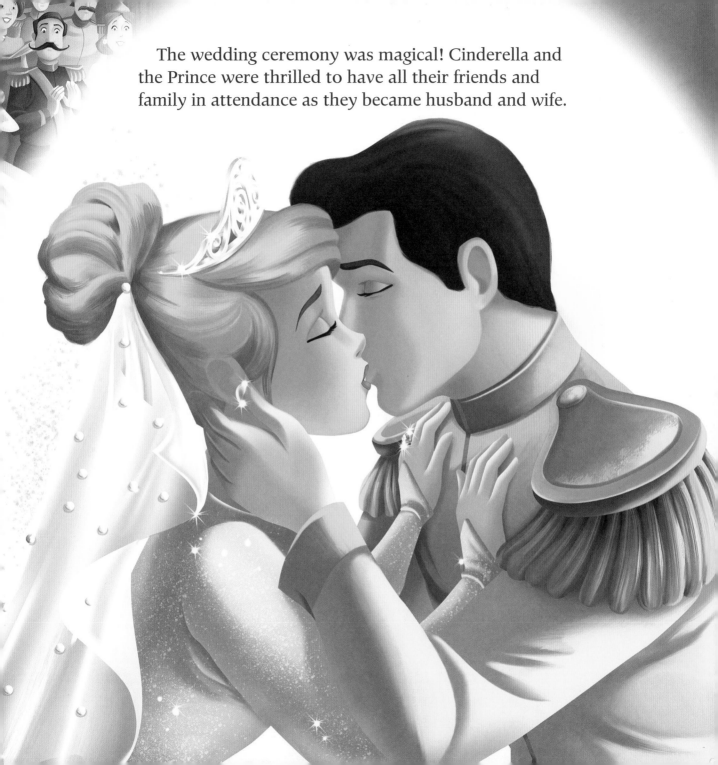

And so, by following tradition—and her heart—
Cinderella had the wedding of her dreams!

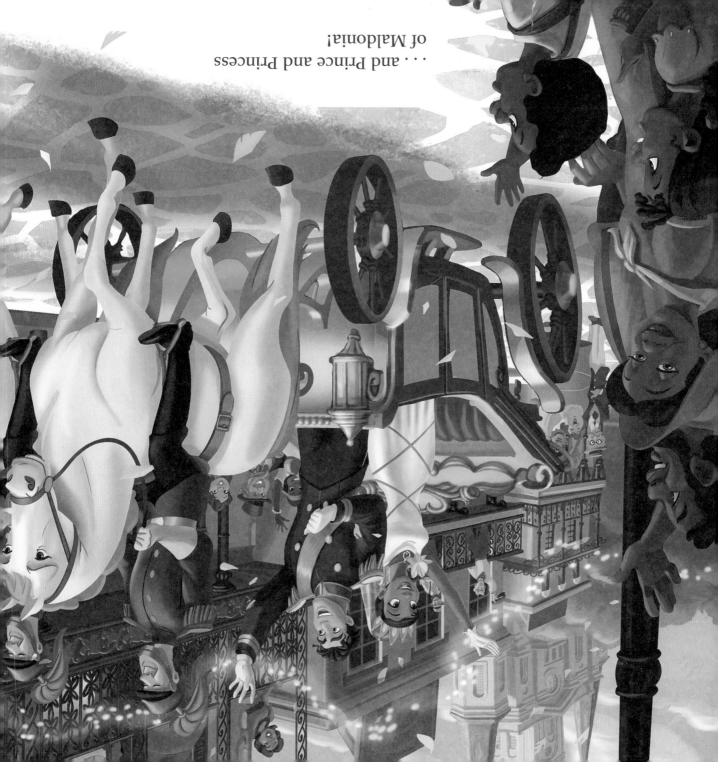

. . . and Prince and Princess
of Maldonia!

A kiss and a promise
made it official: Naveen
and Tiana were husband
and wife . . .

On the big day, Tiana carried
an old spoon of her father's in her
bouquet. She wore the new dress
from her mother, the borrowed
tiara from the Queen, and the
blue necklace from Lottie. All her
loved ones played a part in her
special day!

It was true. Everything did seem perfect. But Tiana missed her father.
The night before her wedding, Tiana looked up at the Evening Star and
realized that her father would always be with her—and she thought of
a way to include him in her wedding.

Soon it was time for Tiana's final wedding gown fitting.
"Your father would be so proud of you," Eudora said
softly. "You've worked hard to make your special day perfect.
And you have remembered what's most important—love."

Just then, Naveen's mother arrived. "Tiana, dear, you may have whatever kind of wedding you wish. I simply hope you will do me the honor of wearing the tiara I wore when I married the King."

Tiana loved the idea!

The royal wedding planners returned early the next morning. But Tiana didn't want them to take charge of her wedding.

"Thank you for all your hard work," she said politely, "but I have made other plans."

"I have something to give you," Charlotte told Tiana. "Now, you know that every bride needs something old, something new, something borrowed, and something blue." She handed Tiana a beautiful necklace. "Here's your 'something blue.'"

Tiana put the necklace on right away. "Thank you, Lottie! It's perfect!"

After everyone else had gone to bed, Tiana and Charlotte sneaked into the kitchen to change the wedding menu.

"There should be a taste of New Orleans," Tiana said. Charlotte agreed.

Outside the room, Tiana's mother, Eudora, had overheard Tiana and Charlotte's conversation. Eudora entered holding a picture of a beautiful gown.

"About your wedding dress," Eudora said. "I may be able to help."

"Mama!" Tiana ran and hugged her. "I am glad to see you!"

"This is so exciting!" Tiana's friend Charlotte exclaimed when the planners finally left.

Tiana sighed. "I had hoped I would get to make my own decisions."

"Tia," Charlotte said, "It's *your* wedding! *You* should plan it."

So Tiana made her first wedding decision. "Lottie, will you be my maid of honor?" Charlotte squealed with delight.

It was almost time for Tiana and Prince Naveen to get married! The royal wedding planners bustled around Tiana with samples of their ideas. Tiana was overwhelmed.

Tiana's Royal Wedding

By Catherine McCafferty

Illustrated by Silvano Scolari and Studio IBOIX

Random House New York

ISBN: 978-0-7364-2910-8

randomhouse.com/kids

MANUFACTURED IN CHINA

10 9 8 7 6 5 4 3 2 1